PAPA PANOV'S SPECIAL CHRISTMAS

Papa Panov's Special Christmas

Leo Tolstoy

A French Folktale by Ruben Saillens
Retold by Leo Tolstoy
Introduction by Shersta Chabot Gatica

Sweetwater Books
An Imprint of Cedar Fort, Inc.
Springville, Utah

ISBN 13: 978-1-59955-919-3

Published by Sweetwater Books, an imprint of Cedar Fort, Inc., 2373 W. 700 S.,
Springville, UT 84663
Distributed by Cedar Fort, Inc., www.cedarfort.com

Cover and page design by Danie Romrell

Printed in the United States of America

10 9 8 7 6 5 4 3 2 1

Printed on acid-free paper

INTRODUCTION

BY SHERSTA CHABOT GATICA

Russian novelist Leo Tolstoy (1828–1910) is best known for his books *War and Peace* and *Anna Karenina*. But before he wrote his famous novels, Tolstoy founded and ran his own school for local peasant children. Subjects taught at the school included reading, arithmetic, history, and creative writing. It is possibly through this experience that Tolstoy developed a bit of a soft spot for telling stories like "Papa Panov's Special Christmas." Originally it was written in French by Ruben Saillens, and Tolstoy translated and adapted this timeless story of a lonely shoemaker who discovers that helping others has its own rewards.

PAPA PANOV'S SPECIAL CHRISTMAS

LEO TOLSTOY

I

IT was Christmas Eve and although it was still afternoon, lights had begun to appear in the shops and houses of the little Russian village, for the short winter day was nearly over. Excited children scurried indoors and now only muffled sounds of chatter and laughter escaped from closed shutters.

Old Papa Panov, the village shoemaker, stepped outside his shop to take one last look around. The sounds of happiness, the bright lights and the faint but delicious smells of Christmas cooking reminded him of past Christmas times when his wife had still been alive and his own children little. Now they had gone. His usually cheerful face, with the little laughter wrinkles behind the round steel spectacles, looked sad now. But he went back indoors with a firm step, put up the shutters and set a pot of coffee to heat on the charcoal stove. Then, with a sigh, he settled in his big armchair.

Papa Panov did not often read, but tonight he pulled down the big old family Bible and, slowly tracing the lines with one forefinger, he read again the Christmas story. He read how Mary and Joseph, tired by their journey to Bethlehem, found no room for them at the inn, so that Mary's little baby was born in the cowshed.

"Oh, dear, oh, dear!" exclaimed Papa Panov, "if only they had come here! I would have given them my bed and I could have covered the baby with my patchwork quilt to keep him warm."

He read on about the wise men who had come to see the baby Jesus, bringing him splendid gifts. Papa Panov's face fell. "I have no gift that I could give him," he thought sadly.

Then his face brightened. He put down the Bible, got up and stretched his long arms to the shelf high up in his little room. He took down a small, dusty box and opened it. Inside was a perfect pair of tiny leather shoes. Papa Panov smiled with satisfaction. Yes, they were as good as he had remembered—the best shoes he had ever made. "I should give him those," he decided, as he gently put them away and sat down again.

He was feeling tired now, and the further he read the sleepier he became. The print began to dance before his eyes so that he closed them, just for a minute. In no time at all Papa Panov was fast asleep.

And as he slept he dreamed. He dreamed that someone was in his room and he knew at once, as one does in dreams, who the person was. It was Jesus.

"You have been wishing that you could see me, Papa Panov," he said kindly. "Then look for me tomorrow. It will be Christmas Day and I will visit you. But look carefully, for I shall not tell you who I am."

When at last Papa Panov awoke, the bells were ringing out and a thin light was filtering through the shutters. "Bless my soul!" said Papa Panov. "It's Christmas Day!"

He stood up and stretched himself for he was rather stiff. Then his face filled with happiness as he remembered his dream. This would be a very special Christmas after all, for Jesus was coming to visit him.

How would he look? Would he be a little baby, as at that first Christmas? Would he be a grown man, a carpenter—or the great King that he is, God's Son? He must watch carefully the whole day through so that he recognized him however he came.

Papa Panov put on a special pot of coffee for his Christmas breakfast, took down the shutters and looked out of the window. The street was deserted, no one was stirring yet. No one except the road sweeper. He looked as miserable and dirty as ever, and well he might! Whoever wanted to work on Christmas Day—and in the raw cold and bitter freezing mist of such a morning?

Papa Panov opened the shop door, letting in a thin stream of cold air. "Come in!" he shouted across the street cheerily. "Come in and have some hot coffee to keep out the cold!"

The sweeper looked up, scarcely able to believe his ears. He was only too glad to put down his broom and come into the warm room. His old clothes steamed gently in the heat of the stove and he clasped both red hands round the comforting warm mug as he drank.

Papa Panov watched him with satisfaction, but every now and then his eyes strayed to the window. It would never do to miss his special visitor.

"Expecting someone?" the sweeper asked at last. So Papa Panov told him about his dream.

"Well, I hope he comes," the sweeper said, "you've given me a bit of Christmas cheer I never expected to have. I'd say you deserve to have your dream come true." And he actually smiled.

When he had gone, Papa Panov put on cabbage soup for his dinner, then went to the door again, scanning the street. He saw no one. But he was mistaken. Someone was coming.

The girl walked so slowly and quietly, hugging the walls of shops and houses, that it was a while before he noticed her. She looked very tired and she was carrying something. As she drew nearer he could see that it was a baby, wrapped in a thin shawl. There was such sadness in her face and in the pinched little face of the baby, that Papa Panov's heart went out to them.

"Won't you come in," he called, stepping outside to meet them. "You both need to warm by the fire and rest."

The young mother let him shepherd her indoors and to the comfort of the armchair. She gave a big sigh of relief.

"I'll warm some milk for the baby," Papa Panov said, "I've had children of my own—I can feed her for you." He took the milk from the stove and carefully fed the baby from a spoon, warming her tiny feet by the stove at the same time.

"She needs shoes," the cobbler said.

But the girl replied, "I can't afford shoes, I've got no husband to bring home money. I'm on my way to the next village to get work."

A sudden thought flashed through Papa Panov's mind. He remembered the little shoes he had looked at last night. But he had been keeping those for Jesus. He looked again at the cold little feet and made up his mind.

"Try these on her," he said, handing the baby and the shoes to the mother. The beautiful little shoes were a perfect fit. The girl smiled happily and the baby gurgled with pleasure.

"You have been so kind to us," the girl said,

when she got up with her baby to go. "May all your Christmas wishes come true!"

But Papa Panov was beginning to wonder if his very special Christmas wish would come true. Perhaps he had missed his visitor? He looked anxiously up and down the street. There were plenty of people about but they were all faces that he recognized. There were neighbors going to call on their families. They nodded and smiled and wished him Happy Christmas! Or beggars—and Papa Panov hurried indoors to fetch them hot soup and a generous hunk of bread, hurrying out again in case he missed the Important Stranger.

All too soon the winter dusk fell. When Papa Panov next went to the door and strained his eyes, he could no longer make out the passers-by. Most were home and indoors by now anyway. He walked slowly back into his room at last, put up the shutters, and sat down wearily in his armchair.

So it had been just a dream after all. Jesus had not come.

Then all at once he knew that he was no longer alone in the room.

This was not a dream, for he was wide awake. At first he seemed to see before his eyes the long stream of people who had come to him that day. He saw again the old road sweeper, the young mother and her baby and the beggars he had fed. As they passed, each whispered, "Didn't you see me, Papa Panov?"

"Who are you?" he called out, bewildered.

Then another voice answered him. It was the voice from his dream—the voice of Jesus.

"I was hungry and you fed me," he said. "I was naked and you clothed me. I was cold and you warmed me. I came to you today in every one of those you helped and welcomed."

Then all was quiet and still. Only the sound of the big clock ticking. A great peace and happiness seemed to fill the room, overflowing Papa Panov's heart until he wanted to burst out singing and laughing and dancing with joy.

"So he did come after all!" was all that he said.

The Holy Bible, KJV. Matthew 25:34–36, 40

THEN shall the King say unto them on his right hand, Come, ye blessed of my Father, inherit the kingdom prepared for you from the foundation of the world:

For I was an hungred, and ye gave me meat: I was thirsty, and ye gave me drink: I was a stranger, and ye took me in:

Naked, and ye clothed me: I was sick, and ye visited me: I was in prison, and ye came unto me.

And the King shall answer and say unto them, Verily I say unto you, Inasmuch as ye have done it unto one of the least of these my brethren, ye have done it unto me.

REFERENCES

Bob Blaisdell and Christopher Edgar, eds., *Tolstoy as Teacher: Leo Tolstoy's Writings on Education* (New York: Teachers & Writers Collaborative, 2000), I.

"20 Famous Christmas Stories," OSR Articles. http://osr.org/en-us/christmas/20-famous-christmas-stories/

0 26575 59193 4